The Shangri-La Shack Literary Arts Journal

Volume 2, Issue 1

The Shangri-La Shack Literary Arts Journal
Volume 2, Issue 1

ISBN: 978-1-105-84930-5

Editor: Deanna Askin
Cover Artwork: Coexistence by Willy Conley
Back Cover Artwork: Heart by Emily K. Bright

Acknowledgements: Thank you to Trina who inspired the production of this journal and to God for granting all of these talented artists their unique gifts of expression.

Published by The Shangri-La Shack™
P.O. Box 99206
San Diego, CA 92169
www.TheShangrilaShack.com
info@theshangrilashack.com

Visit our website **www.TheShangrilaShack.com** for the full-color, online edition and for ordering information.

The Shangri-La Shack Literary Arts Journal is a biannual print and online publication of The Shangri-La Shack, a natural lifestyles organization that promotes happiness and appreciation of our world by bringing together artistic expression, meaningful workshops, natural products, uplifting events, and information sharing in a welcoming venue. The journal provides a stage for creative writing and visual art from an eclectic group of artists that reflect on the real value of our everyday world. This edition features strong themes of nature and wildlife, personal development, memories and aging, and spirituality. We deeply thank everyone who submitted their creative works to this journal. Following is a collection of the pieces that we thought most genuinely expressed the values of The Shangri-la Shack. Come hang out in "the shack" and express, celebrate, reflect, and indulge in the spectacular quirks, gifts, and challenges of our world.

Contents

Internal Mechanisms 1
By Valentina Cano
Photo By Nathan Healy *1*
Crayfish 2
By Yvette A. Schnoeker-Shorb
Dynamics 3
By Lance Nizami
Punishment *By Eleanor Bennet* *3*
Finding Hidden Beauty 4
By Richard Peake
Staying on Course 5
By Yvette A. Schnoeker-Shorb
A Lifetime 6
By Cynthia Ris
Miller's Beach *By Willy Conley* *7*
Spring Detox 8
By Mira Martin-Parker
Weed 9
By Mira Martin-Parker
Autumn Approach *By Willy Conley* *9*
Up Close You Know *By Leah Givens* *10*
The Last Exotic Petting Zoo 11
By Jessica Tyner
Beholder's Eye 12
By Richard Peake
Any Moment Now 13
By Patty Somlo
Creatures *By Eleanor Bennet* *18*
Thank God for the Cocoon 19
By Crystal Lane Swift
What If 20
By Kathryn Lynch
Twelve Steps to Freedom 21
By Kathryn Lynch
Schubert Music Meditation 22
By Francis DiClemente
Hyhyhy *By Eleanor Bennet* *23*
Song of the Old Pueblo 24
By Karen Hugg

Salt From My Eyes 26
By Richard Hartwell
Keeler Beach, Keeler, California *By Lance Nizami* *26*
Escapist 27
By Richard Hartwell
At the Memorial Park 28
By Kirby Wright
Hopscotch, 1918 29
By Bob Meszaros
Shift in Perspective 30
By Kaye Linden
Remembering Edward Brown 31
By John Cullen
I'm Thankful to Wake Up *By Nina Snowden* *33*
Hereafter 34
By Don Kunz
She Awoke to Sunlight *By Emily K. Bright* *36*
Mac and Betsy 37
By Jon Kolb
Bamboo Scoops *By Willy Conley* *42*
EsCAPET *By Sarah Katharina Kayß* *48*
Touch 49
By Cynthia Ris
The Sheep and the Shepherd 50
By Matthew Popadiuk
With Each Step You Take 51
By Matthew Popadiuk
What Becomes of the Fallen Angels? 52
By Mary Shanley
Sea Out *By Eleanor Bennet* *54*
Contributor Profiles 55

Cover Artwork: Coexistence by Willy Conley
Back Cover Artwork: Heart by Emily K. Bright

Internal Mechanisms

By Valentina Cano

There's a book flapping in my head.
Its pages are a whisper of wings,
a pigeon cooing on an attic window,
a grackle and its midnight voice
a triumph of violence.
The book flips open at random,
allowing me peeks of scenery,
all cardboard and cables,
all costumed couples and wings
covered in mildewed dust.
I sneeze at my own thoughts.
I shut my head up;
a puff of dandruffed nonsense
flung to the air.

Photo By Nathan Healy

Crayfish

By Yvette A. Schnoeker-Shorb

I know I should pay
more attention to social
justice, to sustainability,
to community, to small-group
mammalian propensities,
but the perfect symmetry
of this dull green, drying
crayfish is distracting.

The mud-dusted crustacean,
almost hidden in drought-
dropped cottonwood leaves,
brings me to my knees
for a closer look.
The feeler-waving fellow,
facing the wrong way,
is such a distance
from the pond,
indeed from an ancestry
non-native to the past
ecology of this land.

In the moment shared,
I feel the barriers
to that strange and ancient
communitas among creatures
fold, sense the little soul
is dying, and wonder
how any of us survives
our maladaptive drives.

Dynamics

By Lance Nizami

Einstein slept here often, reads the plaque
And photos black-and-white adorn the walls
Where physicist and wife fled to the warmth
Of beckoning desert sun

Where, past large French doors, are bright red bursts -
Flowers probed by tongues thin, hummingbirds
Hovering unconcerned, quite ignorant
That their own flitting tiny grams of mass
Make moving dimples in the warp of space

These wonders have no tension over tensors
And, nested for their quiet evening sleep,
They dream not of the rush to speed of light

But dream they do, and on through night, imagine
Their moving bodies sped from flower to flower
Accelerating effortless left-right
Movements that would seem to bend time-space
And bring a smile upon old Einstein's face.

Punishment *By Eleanor Bennet*

Finding Hidden Beauty

By Richard Peake

Like a shadow moving through brush,
a small creature eludes scrutiny
of a boy using old binoculars.
Following growth on the ditch bank,
this chase continues for what seems hours
until the skulker lights on a branch,
revealing a pastel sparrow
crest raised, an inquiring gazer
who can't resist a closer look
at the binocular bug eyes
of the creature chasing it.
The boy eyes the buffy breast band
on the delicately lined breast,
its stickpin, the soft grayish face.
Knowing this creature new to him
causes trembling excitement
as he thumbs pages of his guide
for the picture he remembers.
Finally, there it is, the bird
flies from the page—Lincoln's sparrow,
not thought to be here, the book says,
not wintering in Virginia,
but there it is, still sitting where
light reveals its muted colors,
a quiet charm always thrilling him
whenever Guy meets it again
to imbibe its pale soft beauty
as he shares with others the knowledge
this secretive, furtive sparrow
spends its winters in concealment
where they have never thought to look.

Staying on Course

By Yvette A. Schnoeker-Shorb

Northbound, they sharply glide
in perfect formation. Dark and light
feathered darts with honks sounding
nationless transition—transportation
without passports. We watch them

from below, our fragile, flightless
bodies perched in a rented, locked box
rolling gracelessly on wheels, pushing
territorial edges—navigating home,
then Mexico, home again, then

Canada—envying the visa-less geese
with their neutral takeoffs and landings
that don't require admittance, work
permits, proof of citizenship. We expect
yet push boundaries, a dilemma

of the mentally homeless, roots soiled
by restlessness or necessity, grounded
by a car with a compass to validate
that, yes, we are headed to Alaska,
a thermometer on the dash to confirm

it is indeed icy outside, and a device
with a voice to direct us confidently
to our destination if we forget how
to read natural features or road maps.
Set on full flight, we have no sense

of place, only of self, technological
narcissists who stare out the window
at a pond that reflects those birds
have surpassed us, landing for night
and leaving us stranded in motion.

A Lifetime

By Cynthia Ris

—After a photograph of macaws in flight from National Geographic Magazine

They look, these macaws, like daredevils shot from two cannons,
their cherry tomato red heads, shoulders edged in green,

a streak of scarlet in each tail, the rest of their feathers shades of brilliant
blue, the forest a blur behind them: he, I imagine, with wings flung out

and higher than his body, looks like he's still gliding from the explosion,
while she, above and slightly behind, dips one wing as she flaps to get ahead,

perhaps pregnant with the extra weight that makes it harder to keep up,
one of the only ways her life might differ from his. These mates-for-life

spend almost every minute together, searching out a clay lick to pick over,
minerals found there, along with fruit and seeds, what they'll share

as well as every chore, every flight, the raising of every chick, finding
every scarce place to nest and protect themselves and their young

as the rains fall and fall and the sun blazes down. Sixty years of paired events,
as long as couples emblazoned on the "LifeStyle" sections of hometown news-

papers, who share secrets of how they stayed married for so long while others
gave up, wore out, stepped out, or were trampled under. Some sound tailor-
made

for the feathery couple: "Parent together," or "Deal with adversity together."
Others less easy for the winged pair: "Forgive one another," "Continue to build
intimacy,

sexually and emotionally." Perhaps the whimsy of flight mutes all arguments;
the intimacy: what happens when day after day, minute after minute,

every palm nut cracked, every chick groomed, every fight to regain their nest
start
and end wing to wing. What builds: the year they spent choosing each other,
the year

spent cementing their bond, layered by action—escape that boa or this human,
puff up and rest, start again as the sun slivers once more through the canopy.

Still they fly—on and on, twenty thousand cycles of moon and sun,
rest and flight, moment by moment, wing by wing. What we don't call love.

Miller's Beach *By Willy Conley*

Spring Detox

By Mira Martin-Parker

I am not candles that are deeply nourishing and rejuvenating. I am not a naturopathic herbalist in beige linen. I am not wild, hand-crafted ingredients, with freshly picked rose hips and essential oils to support your system. I am not a lemon verbena serenity formula. I am not kava kava, with antioxidants and salt and pepper to taste. I am not the expectoration of mud and a quick fizz. I am not a travel friendly wellness boost to the immune system, while promoting a restful sleep. No, that, I am definitely not. I am not a blend of the herb astragalus and elderberry extract. Don't for a minute believe that I am an adrenal regulator, too talented to be underemployed by artisans in Lima. I have never been dyed with flowers and leaves and roots. I will not modulate your blood sugar, with songs and seasonal scents and festive lights. If someone should ever come to you and say, "Never be without your B vitamins and your aroma naturals," know that it is not me who has said this to you. And, if someone should ever come to you offering pure plant and flower wool and yak down using old world methods that are socially conscious, with an organic cotton velvet pillow, know this, that these gifts are not from me. And, if someone should say to you, that a portion of the proceeds will go to protect the planet, that is not me either. And if they should further offer you goat milk soaps that are one with nature, and organic green tea, and organic honey, with essences of plants, turn away from them, dear one, turn away. And know this, none of this is from me.

Weed

By Mira Martin-Parker

A weed. A scrawny, little weed. A weed everyone wanted to kill. A tough, persistent, stalky thing, that kept coming back and coming back, even though it kept getting stepped on over and over again. Swore at over and over again. Called ugly over and over. Pulled out, starved, and poisoned, over and over again. But back it kept coming. Up through the cracks. Without water, or care; just sun and rain, and then back up, again and again, it kept coming. This weed. This scrawny, scratchy thing. Not sweet smelling. Not brightly colored. Just tough and persistent, back again and again. Up through the cracks, again and again, until one day a small yellow flower poked its head out from underneath one of the leaves, and God smiled at it and said, "Finally you made it through, little one. I was hoping to see you!"

Autumn Approach *By Willy Conley*

Up Close You Know *By Leah Givens*

The Last Exotic Petting Zoo

By Jessica Tyner

In the dripping cold of an Oregon January,
miasma of wet dog clung to us like a
discarded lover. You, sick
with a cough and a heavy head tucked
in the pages of a book. I drove
like hell down the coastal
back roads. No one holds tigers
and lions in the winter
but us.
The wanton mud swallowed our shoes,
sucked our feet in searching gulps
while the animals watched.
You held her,
bristled paws like a kiwano,
as I cradled the bottle of milk
into her frantic mouth, knowing you'll never
think me as magnificent as you
do right now.
I gifted you a tiger cub, her claws etching
delicate scars into your forearms,
while the rain scoured us to the bone.

Beholder's Eye

By Richard Peake

Not so beautiful
as Botticelli's Venus rising
from the Adriatic Sea,
at dockside in San Francisco
a harbor seal
pops out of dark water
onto the jetty rocks
greeting her sunning friends
with grunts of harsh hello
made emphatic with the slap
of a flipper on the stones.
They wait there near the dock
expectantly hoping for a fish
or some other dainty seafood
thrown out by admiring hands.
Not every connoisseur of beauty
demands a svelte mermaid
or a gorgeous goddess
to mesmerize
the searching eye.

Any Moment Now

By Patty Somlo

On a bright, warm afternoon in late October, Miriam Larson, Ph.D. from the University of California Berkeley, stood surrounded by turquoise, yellow and chartreuse green one-story buildings in the central plaza of Angangueo. High in the Mexican mountains, bordered by once-thick forests that had come dangerously close to disappearing, Dr. Larson waited. The previous year, she had stood in this very same place, and every year before that, going back a good three decades.

She had on a large, floppy canvas hat with an overdeveloped brim, knotted under her chin as a precaution against an excessively forceful burst of wind. The beige khaki hat was frayed, and what hat wouldn't have been after three decades? Dr. Larson had worn the broken umbrella-shaped hat for every one of the more than thirty butterfly migrations she had witnessed. Never in a million years would Miriam Larson have revealed this fact to her department colleagues or experts tenured in other universities. But she fervently believed that the velvety black, yellow and white butterflies strained their tiny eyes in search of her hat, the last thirty minutes of their remarkable journey.

The hat normally sat centered on Miriam's head. Today, though, the cotton khaki material tipped ever so slightly to the left. The brim was crumpled, like a sheet of paper headed for the trash. If this didn't indicate that life was not as it should be for Dr. Larson, she also had on two left-foot sandals. The pink flesh of her right foot was leaking over the outer edge of one. Both sandals were brown, since the professor tended to buy shoes of the same color and style, for no reason other than that it made life's choices a great deal simpler. Equally revealing, she had neglected the last hole when buttoning her blouse. As a result, the light blue cotton sleeveless blouse hung diagonally across her torso.

Until this past spring, butterflies had been Miriam Larson's all-consuming passion. She had researched every aspect of their annual journey – the remarkable fifty-mile-per-day rate during their thousand-plus mile flight from Canada to Mexico; the internal compass that kept them on course, even on days when clouds hid their normal guide, the orbit of the sun; their winter hibernation in the Mexican mountains, and mating pressed softly against warm tree bark; not to mention the births and deaths of several generations on their return flight north. When the first evidence surfaced that, like so many species, Dr. Larson's beloved butterflies were becoming endangered; she found it hard to concentrate. Some days, she had to remind herself to eat.

But, it was an event in Dr. Larson's immediate life that rattled her equilibrium and sent a crack squirreling through her once solidly work-obsessed life. Dr. Miriam Larson, whose butterfly studies and field trips comprised the passion and purpose of her life, had begun to lose her eyesight.

Like her increasingly waning vision, the die-off of the butterflies had not happened overnight. For years, the forests surrounding Angangueo had been cut, leaving bare swathes with little protection from the cold and wind for those heavenly creatures, whose wings looked as if they'd been brushed by a master Japanese painter. More butterflies died. Only three years before, limp, dark wings had fallen from the trees into hopeless, frigid clumps. The sight forced Miriam to crouch down and vomit, right there on the ground.

Of course, her beloved butterflies and her eyesight weren't the only things that had quietly begun to expire in Miriam Larson's life. So too had her ability to sit long hours in the lab, peering through a microscope, or to stand on her feet presenting papers at academic conferences. From the bunions on her big toes to the fallen arches, her feet ached at night. Her eyesight failed her in low light.

It was at night when she'd first noticed a darkening around the outer edges of her eyes. The doctor performed a quick laser surgery that seemed to help for a time. But, the darkening returned and now affected Miriam's vision even in the daytime. She began to appear in the hallways of the science building wearing an oversized pair of oval tortoiseshell glasses. Whenever students spoke to her in class, they felt as if they were looking through a series of prisms sitting on top of her eyes.

Miriam stood in the plaza shielding her eyes. This was the moment for which she waited. She turned her gaze from right to left. The little turquoise tienda where she bought cold lemon-lime sodas, the bottles thick and heavy in her hand, sat to her right, which meant she was facing north. The questions arose. Would they arrive? How many would come? And, once here, would they survive?

Dark walls circled the outer edges of her eyes. To see better, she needed to swivel her entire body from left to right. The sky was a deep blue, empty of clouds. Empty, too, of butterflies, so far.

She chewed on her bottom lip, a habit she'd tried to cure but which lately had begun to resurface. She searched the sky another time. In that moment, she let herself imagine things were as they had been the year she first came to Angangueo. She pretended that she suddenly saw a darkening, not caused by her narrowing sight, but by the butterflies eclipsing the sun and the bright clear sky.

Her breath caught, and she felt the lump that had started to appear too often in her throat. She dropped her head down, as she fought back the tears. What bothered her most was that all these years she had been fine, perfectly fine. Of course, it had been hard to watch the trees surrounding this village disappear. She had gone with the scientists and young environmentalists as they met with villagers in the neighboring towns. They had told stories of poor peasants, like themselves, being murdered; their mutilated bodies hung from the few remaining trees, as a warning from those who came in the night and illegally chopped down and hauled out the trees. She had watched, year after year, as the ranks of butterflies returning to Angangueo thinned. She had even let the thought enter her mind that, one day, not a single butterfly might return.

Yes, Miriam Larson had had her moments of grief and despair. She had wrestled with a fierce hopelessness that everything beautiful and mysterious was on the verge of disappearing. Perhaps, if her beloved butterflies had still been cheerfully mating and reproducing, her heart might have been able to accept her shrinking sight. But then she managed to straighten her back and lift her eyes to the sky.

Miriam had never been a religious woman, but those silken wings propelling infinitely millions of fragile creatures down the North American continent caused her to believe in a force that could only be described as holy. She, herself, migrated to Mexico like a homing pigeon, because those fluttering wings made her spirit flush with a hopefulness she couldn't construct sentences to adequately describe.

In some recent years, the bright blue mountain sky had refused to darken with clouds of black, yellow and white wings. Butterflies eventually sputtered in, but only in sparse, bedraggled groups who came to die. Miriam studied the sky with a cautious optimism but knew something in her heart at the same time. Even if the butterflies returned in clouds so black and huge they blocked out the sun, the ecstasy she had felt every year for the past thirty would never return to light up Miriam's life.

Moments after the sun set, light was instantly swallowed by a startlingly dark sky. Miriam twisted her neck, to relieve the stiffness from leaning back too long. Scattered street lights were flicked on. Miriam took slow careful steps, her fading eyes fixed on the ground.

She had waited for three days, surveying the sky. Not one single butterfly had arrived. She refused to believe this might be the end. If it was, whatever would she do with her life? Even though she'd eaten only a handful of sunflower seeds and a small box of raisins for lunch, Miriam had no appetite. Her room in the hospedaje had such low light she found it impossible to read, even though the print in her book was several inches larger than normal. Better to walk carefully in the dark, than to return to close her eyes and wait for sleep that wouldn't come.

Miriam raised her head for a moment, just as a terrible wave of self-pity washed over her. Why had she made so little of her life? Yes, she had produced a few unimportant books and articles, but no great discoveries. No groundbreaking research that would live on once Miriam completely lost her sight or, eventually, when she was gone. Worst of all, there had been little she'd contributed to save her beloved butterflies.

As if that wasn't distressing enough, Miriam began to wonder what she'd missed by never falling in love. And would her life have been more fulfilled if she'd had a child? Why, until these last few months with her ever-shrinking field of vision growing narrower, none of this had entered her mind. Her father, a busy cardiologist, had raised Miriam after her mother died. Miriam had grown up assuming that being occupied day and night with her own thoughts was a perfectly normal life.

Miriam suddenly looked up and noticed the lights. She walked closer, for some reason drawn to that spot. The cemetery was lit with flickering candles and the white glare of flashlights. People were gathered in small groups around the gravesites.

Sprigs of purple and pink bougainvillea spilled from vases set atop colorful tablecloths on the ground. One young man strummed a battered guitar and sang a mournful tune about butterflies and lost love. Children ran laughing amongst the graves and people smiled. The air smelled of corn tortillas and burnt wood.

"Señora," a voice said, and Miriam turned in that direction. It was the owner of the little tienda where Miriam bought bottled water and sodas. "Come, sit with us and have something to eat," he said.

Miriam stepped over to where the man was standing surrounded by plates of food. Several women wrapped in blue, red and yellow blankets sat on the ground with the children. One of the women nodded to Miriam, then piled some chicken smothered in a dark sauce, rice and beans on a plate and handed it to the professor, who was still standing off to the side.

The food was heavenly and Miriam realized that she was starving. For the first time in days, she felt all right. Every so often, the store owner, Gilberto, smiled at her, and then looked at his children tumbling on the tablecloth.

"The butterflies," Gilberto suddenly said.

"Not yet," Miriam answered, though the question hadn't been raised.

"I believe they will come," Gilberto said. "They are our ancestors. We have food for them and are here, all of us, waiting. Any moment now, they will arrive."

Miriam didn't respond but thought, I wish I could feel so hopeful. Gilberto looked at Miriam and nodded. "They have always come back to us. Yes, some bad people have taken advantage, but we are guarding the trees now. What would we do, we say to one another, without the visits from our loved ones? They help us to be brave and strong, to fight those who only look out for themselves."

Miriam smiled and nodded, glad to be in such warm company. If she were a butterfly, she thought, she would certainly want to come and be here with these kind people.

The guitar player stopped strumming and the chatter in the cemetery suddenly quieted. Children quit giggling and wrestling each other to the ground.

The first butterfly dropped onto the gravestone of Gilberto's grandmother. A second came down on the head of a small child. In moments, the cemetery was filled with wings, fluttering so fast, a person watching couldn't glimpse more than a blur of yellow and black.

Miriam stayed very still, while bathing in the fleeting rapture of the butterflies' return. Then she felt the wings dust her eyelashes. She, of course, could not see, as they brushed her nose and cheeks, her chin and finally her lips. Eventually, the little creatures settled themselves, in the narrow crevasses, to the left and right of her eyes.

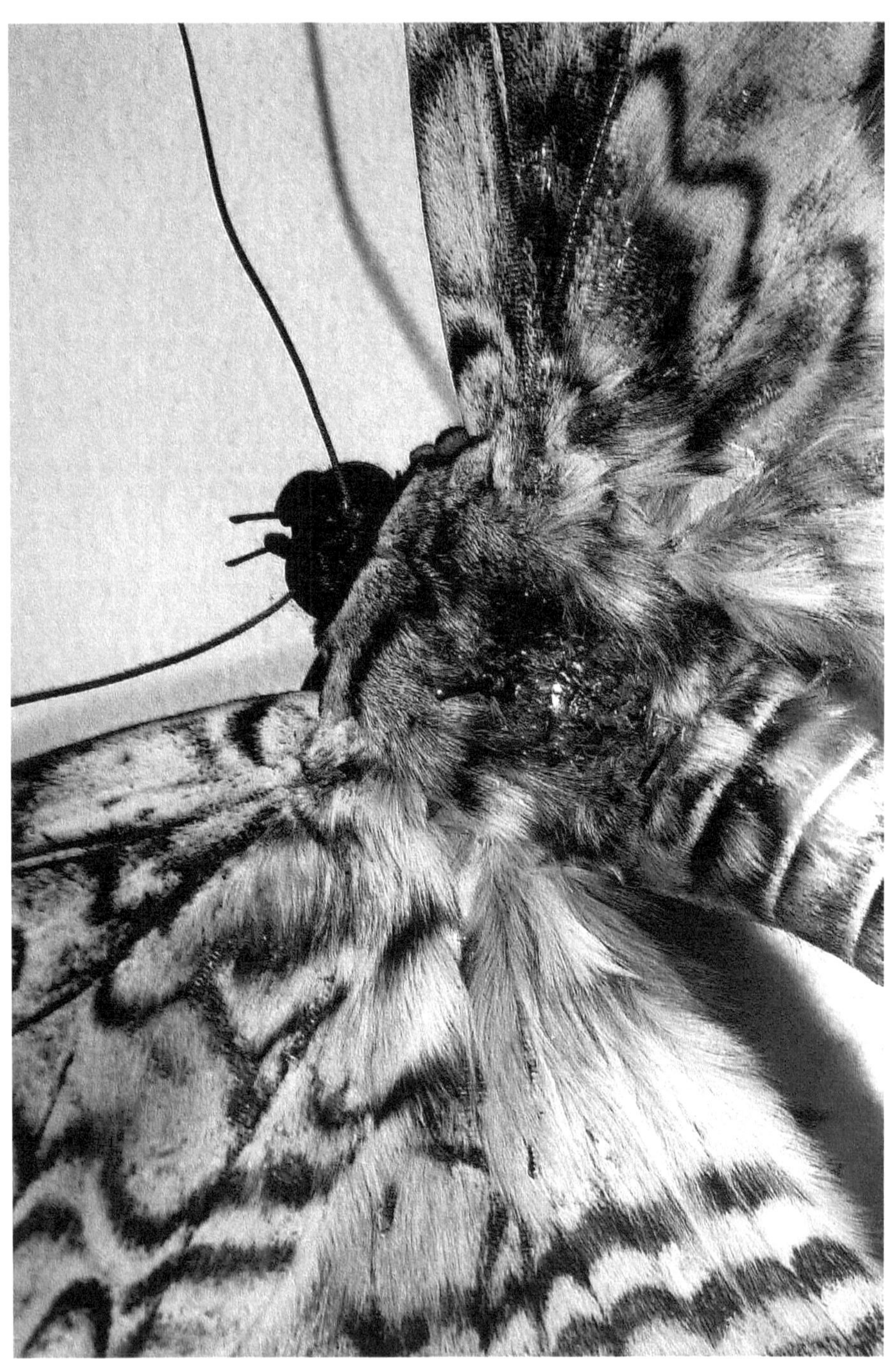

Creatures *By Eleanor Bennet*

Thank God for the Cocoon

By Crystal Lane Swift

She was born among calla lilies and roses
Surrounded by sunlight and fragrance
Then came the cocoon
Wrapped tight around her plump body
And she flapped
God made her so that her wings would strengthen as she struggled
As she grew, she took a breath and struggled
A bird came and pecked at the cocoon
A cat pawed and hissed
She kept flapping
They told her to cut her hair
They told her to change her image
She kept flapping
Some veins broke
A sprain and a fracture
She kept flapping
They raped her
And everyone called her a liar
She tried to drink it all away
And I kept flapping
When I emerged, I was covered in scars, wings pierced and imperfect
But I can fly
I flapped and flapped
I beat my wings until they bled
And I thank God for the cocoon

What If

By Kathryn Lynch

What if I'd never drank or picked up a drug?
Instead of a beating, what if I'd got a hug?
What if I'd waited instead of having sex?
What if the planks in my eyes were just specks?
What if my friends didn't turn against me?
What if I had understood the meaning of free?
What if there had been someone who heard and understood?
What if I had just done right and acted like I should?
What if I had understood the meaning of love?
What if I'd believed there really was a God above?
What if Dad was faithful? What if he'd stayed?
What if I'd been open and honest, not afraid?
What if I'd gotten married either time I got engaged?
What if, like my sister, I was outwardly enraged?
What if I'd had the courage to cut it deep enough?
What if I'd broke down instead of always acting tough?
In the mirror, what if I had seen who I really am?
What if I had soared through life and left it all to chance?
What if I had smiled instead of always looking down?
I'd never have become the woman who sits before you now.

Twelve Steps to Freedom

By Kathryn Lynch

The people in here seem to be on a mission.
They talk about promises, steps and traditions.
Will any of it work for me?
I've only gone as far as Step Three.
There's so much truth in the words being spoken,
of willingness and keeping our minds wide open.
Will I be amazed before I'm half-way through?
Am I the only one, or are you scared, too?
Powerless? Yeah, that's why I'm in jail.
I couldn't buy freedom even if I had a bail.
I long for the day when I don't regret my past,
and I'm realizing slowly that feelings don't last.
Feelings — today, I can actually feel.
It's amazing, almost to the point of surreal.
I'm coming to know the true meaning of peace,
and learning how to stand on my own two feet.
I thought I could beat this, but I was wrong.
It's taken people down who were twice as strong.
I know that it's only by God's grace
that instead of six feet under, I came to this place.
Shortcomings? Yes, please take those away.
I'm tired of coming up short day after day.
Amends? I wish I knew where to begin.
I'll start by addressing the issues within.
I no longer hang my head and cower.
I've put my faith in a Higher Power.
I look around at all my new sisters and brothers;
which ones will die so that I can recover?
Will I be able to handle their deaths?
Will they save their souls before they breathe their last breaths?
I cannot help but feel somehow at home,
and I'm finding some comfort in the love being shown.
In my gut, something tells me I'm on the right track,
and with that, I suppose I will keep coming back.

Schubert Music Meditation

By Francis DiClemente

The piano notes of Franz Schubert, playing on Syracuse's Classic FM station, seep through the car radio and wash over me, invading the space of my inner mind. I sit alone in a metal-aluminum box built in Detroit a decade ago and equipped with a rattling engine that announces it age.

It is mid-December in Syracuse, New York, and this afternoon, unlike most days in the last month of the year, it is sunny and bright, above 35 degrees and not a speck of snow covers the grass or this semi-empty mall parking lot. I delight in the sunlight creating sharp delineations between the sky, the ground, the large office building in the distance, and the surrounding countryside dotted with fir trees and spindly, auburn-brown trees with branches devoid of leaves.

As I sit in my car, I listen to the music, watch a seagull circling some lampposts, and let my mind go in meditation of my place in this city, this zip code, this world, this time in history. And without being invited, a dark thought comes to me. I think how easy it would be to let myself slip away, to strap a wide-mouthed plastic hose to the tailpipe and tuck it inside the driver's side window. I could let the small car fill with carbon monoxide and drift off without being noticed by the shoppers heading to the stores or to lunch.

No one would find me for several hours. And later tonight, my car would be the last one left in the parking lot. I would be discovered by a lone security guard doing a sweep of the mall before punching out. Or maybe I wouldn't be spotted until the next morning, when an old lady goes out to walk her white poodle.

Listening to Schubert always awakens in me a sense of spiritual discovery, as if the composer's chords penetrate my ear canals and tickle receptors in the brain that are open to pondering the mystery of human existence.

Today I discover just how easy it would be to discard the life I have been given, to sever my earthly ties, to choke my breath intentionally. And I realize, those prone to questioning our place in the world, those people whom sadness often infects – and I count myself among this group – need ironclad discipline to provoke a desire to fight to stay alive, to not give up, to not submit to the easy way out. They require a survival instinct, a force to help them accept each day regardless of circumstances. This may not be easy, but the alternative is far worse.

We need this will to live even when our lives find us no richer, no happier and no less lonely. We have to let the fragile bubble moments—when this world and the next seem closer in proximity—to glide over and wash away without us being sucked into the maze of self-absorption that can lead to self-destruction.

So today, when the announcer's voice comes on the radio at the end of Schubert's piano piece, I turn off the car engine, saunter across the parking lot, enter the mall, and buy a movie ticket to see Clint Eastwood's J. Edgar. And the Monday afternoon passes without my resistance, and the matinee kills two hours of my life, instead of me killing the man in the driver's seat.

Hyhyhy *By Eleanor Bennet*

Song of the Old Pueblo

By Karen Hugg

In November, the crickets cling to the walls or hide in the cracks of the concrete patio. They spring away at the touch of a human hand. They like the lone shade. They like to hang on the screen door until it slides back, and on the shadow of my chair until it skids when I sit down. I eye the Mourning Dove in the tree. She eyes me; then flaps down to peck on the ground, marching in a little circular pattern that only makes sense to her. The bird lets out a plaintive hoo as it lifts and lands in the Cholla. Now, it's hidden by white spikes on succulent branches, crisscrossing into a fortress of danger for cats, and coyotes, and an unsuspecting gardener who's been poisoned by brushing against a comb.

The work is finished now, but the sun isn't. It still glows like a godly spotlight, illuminating the earth, gathering in its arms all the corners and underneaths and enclosures. The shadows slant away and so does satiation in my stomach. Out front, where I creak the gate shut, the sun shows the asphalt road for what it is and where it goes, melting tar that leads to the big-daddy four-lane street of blaring horns and flying tanks and traffic, traffic, traffic.

But first the Bermuda Grass lines the curbs like an abandoned runway. The Palo Verde trees sway and drop their dry strands like straw. The litter is a scattered hay of what couldn't get water, what was on the farthest, outermost reach of a branch, or what was in the shade and died because stronger branches took its place above, in the light. In the sky, the dried palm leaves, two-stories up on that tropical pole, flitter in the papery breeze.

From a dead Bougainvillea by the neighbor's door, a man emerges, his hat stained, his body starved, his nails rimmed with the grease of motor oil and chicken fat. "What's that dog?" he says. He points to my dingo. "My brother's got the same one. It's a wolf."

"Did you know," I say, "humanitarian aid is never a crime?" and point to the yard sign next door. He waves and staggers on, heading to the Circle K for his tub of sugar water.

Down the street, on the driveway of the senior couple's home, dead leaves speckle the gravel and I wonder what Mr. Sedan will do when he finds them. Boy, will he be mad. Last week at twilight, he picked up a sole bottle cap, then went inside where the open window showed the Mrs. reading a newspaper. The television flashed a large 44 degrees for the nighttime low. The gravel drive is as it should be now: no visiting RV, no brown leaves, the white rocks raked and dry and exposed to the sun's curve. I wonder how that plastic matchstick screen in the carport hasn't chipped and degraded and blown away. It's been twenty years hanging.

The saguaros listen to the music of the crickets all around us. No wonder a thousand rattlesnakes slink the desert. A million crickets. And dozens of birds who've poked their condo holes in the spiked surface of a saguaro. Tall squishy saguaro. Hard as rock saguaro. Saguaro life. The birds fly and circle, visiting each other's holes and landing their tiny bird feet on the long prickles with an expertise I've never understood. The wee-weep and hoo-hoos and clucking notes chime together like Sonoran bells.

Blocks over, on the four-lane we call a highway, the bus slows and hisses to a stop. A lady with a broken arm is waiting beneath the plastic roof. She steps up inside and disappears from the black spots of gum and dried urine on the sidewalk, the large reddish stain that once ran from the garbage can to the gutter. It will disappear too in the next monsoon. At the Walk button, I wait, studying the public half-wall. It has a mosaic of hands and heart and an odd shape that when you stare at it long enough becomes the shape of Tucson itself. The city is a piece in the puzzle of the Southwest, but who thinks of the boundary? These boundaries don't exist in this natural world; there's no fence or gate to break through to get in or out, just the sand and stars to visit.

The giant cars stop at the white stripes and I cross. Here comes a woman, riding her bike against traffic in the bike lane. I know her, and I don't. She's the one with the homemade trailer with the duct-taped side rails where a heap of metal rods and slumped garbage bag and a three-legged table ride inside. She picks the streets clean every Thursday. Her hair's in a bandana, practical but brimless, and I don't know how her face avoids the burn. As she nears, the tires on the trailer bump and bounce at a broken patch. What's the use of it all, and yet, what a beautiful use. She tools past the idling cars. In this woman I see myself: she's not sure what she'll find where, but knows happy well from where she's come.

Salt From My Eyes

By Richard Hartwell

I'm gliding through the night again,
Beneath a dome of desert stars,
Picking up the souls of dead animals,
Dodging their bloated bodies of the dark,
Alone on the road with my mobile thoughts.

Looking over my shoulder reluctantly,
Expecting to be overtaken at any moment,
Family arguments left in the dusk behind,
Plagues of the lying locust, leftover friction,
Pursue me to the dawn, matching my speed.

In trying to escape into the heat of the desert,
I find that the doom of my regretted words
Reverberates; emotions feel a cooling bellows
Through the open window of my soul, and the
Predators of remorse lick the salt from my eyes.

Keeler Beach, Keeler, California *By Lance Nizami*

Escapist

By Richard Hartwell

Pine-green mountains, needlepoint
Against grey air, blue disappearing,
Likely second-growth trees planted by
Some outfit looking for long-range gains
Not shortsighted like some companies.

When it rains hard on over-cut slopes,
Mud bathes hillside until rivulets run
Into rivers of orange that turn red in my
Dreams, as the land is raped, slashed,
Scraped raw, left to bleed out to death,

Black highway ribbons winding between
Mountains, bordered by fruit orchards,
Vegetable fields; truck gardens for towns
Like Roseburg and Cottage Grove, cities
Like Eugene and Salem, and in between.

These were the plot points on my map,
Work a day or two, make five or ten,
Sometimes more, sometimes less, just
Escape from Coquille, milking cows,
Drinking, fighting, maybe fleeing a girl.

Going north, eventually Portland,
Expecting everything to be better,
Away from the plywood mill and
Outlaw shake-mills, cows, bars,
Orchards, small farms: the bleeding.
Finding no peace, no sense of worth
In Portland, tried Seattle, El Paso,
Others farther flung across mid-belt
America where work could be found,
Until I realize, I only want to go home.

At the Memorial Park

By Kirby Wright

I bring yellow heliconia and red torch ginger.
You're planted on a rise beside the shower tree.
Diamond Head looms in the background.
You're too low to see the ocean.

You're planted on a rise beside the shower tree.
Show people you love 'em when they're alive, you said.
You're too low to see the ocean.
I was your nightmare: a law school flunk out.

Show people you love 'em when they're alive, you said.
You haunt me more than mother.
You're too low to see the ocean.
Chan Yang and Fu Chuan Lee flank you.

I fill your vase to the brim.
Diamond Head looms in the background.
A plover lands on your marker.
I bring yellow heliconia and red torch ginger.

Hopscotch, 1918

By Bob Meszaros

had a little bird
its name was Enza.
opened a window
and in-flu-enza.

The tossing of a flat grey stone on boxes
scratched with sticks into the dirt; the small skips
of retrieval; the leaning down, the straightening up;
the rush, on one leg, to return:

A game of strength and balance, older
than bent rim backboards and bicycle racks,
than strike zones chalked in white on brick.

The game my mother and her sister played
each afternoon behind the Centerville Grammar School,
on a playground empty as the open classroom windows,
in October, a month before the Great War ended.

Shift in Perspective

By Kaye Linden

Forty years past childhood, I climbed the twisty serpentine stairs up to my father's house in the Sydney suburbs, slipping and gripping with my toes to balance on the moss- covered, leaf littered stone stairs I had once skipped over as a child. Glass windows, floor to ceiling, opened onto balconies in front of the house and branches of ghost gums touched the wrought iron railings like tender fingertips curling, limbs and trunks massed together against the light.

Each afternoon, my father sat alone for sugared and creamed tea in rose-patterned china cups passed down from grandparents. The sun could barely whisper through the dense knotted gum trees, centurions gnarled like my grandmother's fingers in morning. We sat staring at our feet, as the forest embraced us with a shrouded fog moving in from the coast, the hint of a cold southeast polar wind and the damp breath of autumn.

His legs crossed one over the other, shifting them on occasion; his blue eyes rheumy now and tearing not from memories lost, but from eighty years of war within and without. He wore his World War II medals on his lapel, brass pins with faded colors.

"How are the kids?" he asked, after two cups of tea.

I nodded, "They're fine. Teenagers. You know how that is."

A puzzled wave passed over his face, and he frowned, "Oh? Do I?"

"I was a teenager once, Dad."

"What's your name again?" He interlaced his old hands and bent forward. "Are you my daughter?"

"Yes, Dad. Harriet."

"I'm having a little trouble remembering," he said. "Did you live with me?"

"I grew up here, Dad. You used to make tea for me at four o'clock every day."

He nodded but bit his lip. "What's your name again?"

A kookaburra screamed from a tall gum tree, and a red rosella swooped down for biscuit crumbs. I felt like Gretel trying to navigate home but sparrows had stolen the clues to a once sunny path. I said goodbye and left.

I re- slipped down the down stairs, and as I waved goodbye to the shadowed man on the balcony, the fifty stone steps of my childhood merged into the reality of only ten stone steps of today, steep steps remembered from years ago through a small child's eyes.

Remembering Edward Brown

By John Cullen

Saturday visits to Green View Manor, rhythms
difficult to capture or touch. Men
in shirts ballooning sizes too large, slumped
on a sofa watching Wheel of Fortune, faces
stretched as plants after light, and the overfed beagle
suffering in the heat. A flat-toned voice complained
down a hall. Things moved so slowly
I felt the urge to run but sat in his room
to share the local gossip.
The Hansen's shepherd killed a rabbit.
Robert Mickelson danced a jig
at Ellen's wedding. Joe Turner wouldn't speak
of his brother's stroke. Last weekend
we cut the trumpet vine that overhung the arbor.
Finally, stories exhausted, we'd gaze
outside at the piles of cinders
and splintering ties. Or sometimes, midsentence,
he'd demand his leg and strap it on to pace
the room, the way for years with Allegheny Freight
he'd pulled his watch and met all trains.
That last year, though, often I found him staring,
listening, perhaps, to the Allegheny's ghost
burn coal to steam the eastern line.
Or maybe to memories
of another America, where retired men lived
fixing broken clocks, and paid the local boys
to lower storms each spring.
He's been dead ten years,
and on that sun drenched day no one shivered
at the fake green carpet he'd certainly have hated
or stared down the nest where coffin met earth.
Just one or two friends. A cousin from Missouri,
who clearly feared I expected some inheritance
or planned a way to contest his will.
But today he's alive, if only in memory,
losing his leg in public for a joke,
hoeing rows of cabbage in his backyard garden,

or standing in a corner of his Michigan basement
brewing homemade wine from dandelion or cherry.

There may have been a dark heart in his past,
a rainy afternoon he left a dog chained out,
a day he failed to give the local wino change,
or made someone he loved take the long way home.
For all I know, he may have done worse.
But no matter what he said or did, I'd rather not hear it.
I'll remember best the man he was; full
of trains and basement brew, never at a loss
to offer a hand, and always ready
with an armload of cabbage
or with stories of war, or a shiny nickel
he'd polished to perfection for one child's pleasure.

I'm Thankful to Wake Up *By Nina Snowden*

Hereafter

By Don Kunz

He had his best conversations with her after she was dead.

When she died, he did all the usual things — weep, curse God, turn her into a major saint. His wife had been sensitive to the needs of others, nurturing, and a spectacular cook. She was also overweight, stubborn, and, at times, a shrew. Like most husbands he got what he deserved.

He was intensely antisocial; an angry man given to fits of temper and moroseness. His happiest moments were spent alone and so went unobserved. Every year, he took his one-month summer vacation alone in some small town in the mountains of Colorado, always a different town. He packed enthusiastically, unable to conceal his glee at escaping the heat and humidity of Kansas, of leaving without her. She took this as an affront and punished him for it when he returned.

Separate vacations made obvious what had been true for years. As they had aged, their characters and preferences had become so decided that neither could compromise. He went west; she went east. He liked country music at top volume. She preferred classical and opera just above the threshold of hearing. He enjoyed exercise; she avoided it. He hungered for red meat; she became a vegetarian. He quit smoking; she refused. Cumulatively, these small differences became large. The familiarity of marriage tore away the polite courtesies, which disguise conflicts between friends. They were no longer lovers. Sometimes they were enemies.

In middle age they had talked of divorce, done marital counseling, and finally settled into a fragile truce. They tolerated one another. They felt bound by history. She loved the bungalow they had built when Shawnee Mission was still a suburb and wanted to live in it the rest of her life, hosting dinner parties for her many friends, holiday celebrations with family, and monthly meetings with her bridge group.

Returning home from work each evening, he became more and more convinced that their bungalow resembled a mid-western funeral parlor. He wanted to sell it, bank the money, and retreat to a small town where he could live frugally, reliving his impoverished childhood in North Dakota. He dreamed of moving every six months — before acquaintances could assume the privileges and intimacies to which friendship might entitle them. His idea of a social life was bantering with waitresses at truck stops.

To compensate for his summer vacations without her, she took weeklong trips with her bridge group three times a year. The eight women friends had been together for seventeen years. They would drive to St. Louis or the Lake of the Ozarks, stay in a luxurious hotel, eat at elegant restaurants, and then sit smoking and drinking and telling off-color jokes while they played cards. On such a trip to Branson, Missouri one late fall, her smoker's cough worsened. She was playing no trump, running out a long string of hearts when she was convulsed by a fit of violent coughing. She saw her handkerchief was speckled with blood.

X-rays. MRIs. Surgery. Chemotherapy. Radiation. Four months later she was dead. When she was gone, he had no antagonist against whom to declare what he stood for. Without intending to, she had given his existence shape and significance. If she had not been such a homebody, he could have left the traffic-clogged, heavily industrialized, polluted urban sprawl where they lived, then rambled about in the pure country air as he wished. If she hadn't been so materialistic, he could have escaped the burden of a house full of furniture, a mortgage, and two cars. If she had not been so gregarious, he could have avoided spending all those evenings feigning good cheer while playing host to a circle of contemptible acquaintances. If it hadn't been for her, he could have left his depressing job as an accountant, retired early, and lived cheaply.

After she was gone, he could do anything he wanted. That made him angry, angrier than before. He bitterly resented losing the barrier he had erected to his happiness, and, having spent much of his married life convincing himself he was miserable, he began to search for another reason to be so. At first, he punished himself with guilt for having projected his own shortcomings upon her. But, finally, he found it most satisfying to embrace the noble stereotype of grieving widower. After a decade of blaming his wife in life, he began to celebrate her in death.

She became beautiful in his memory. He resurrected her from a computer box full of snapshots. Every evening he traced her evolution from Raytown High School through their married life and found her loveliness growing less fresh, but more profound — something in the eyes and posture that made him overlook the thickening of her body and wrinkling of her face. She became the genial hostess of a hundred celebrations graced by laughter and generous portions, flowers and candles and seasonal decorations, family embraces and photographs.

She became the best wife that had ever lived; the best mother in the history of the world. She became someone worthy of epic mourning — daily visits to the grave site, late night phone calls to their grown children (the son in Denver, the daughter in San Jose), fits of weeping over glasses of red wine. Now that she was dead, he could do all those things, which he had convinced himself she had prevented. And he told himself he would, but he was too grief stricken at present. A man who had lost the best wife in the world could not afford to be so self-indulgent.

He began talking to her almost constantly. He talked to her as he sat rocking in the bentwood chair in the family room, where he had laid the gray slate floor and whitewashed the casement-window frames. He talked to her at her graveside overlooking the small pond at Prairie Lea Cemetery, while he arranged cut tulips in a crystal vase. He talked to her in the musty basement when he lifted dumbbells. He talked to her in their early American king-sized bed, as the nights grew longer. He promised her he would change nothing. He knew that was the way she would have wanted it hereafter.

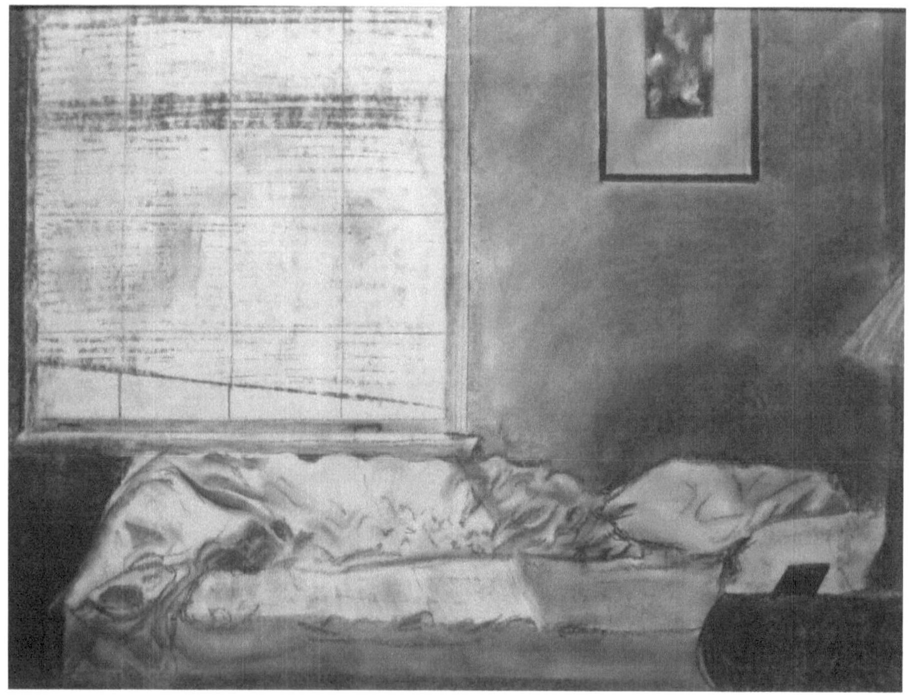

She Awoke to Sunlight *By Emily K. Bright*

Mac and Betsy

By Jon Kolb

I was sitting on the brand new deck of my neighbor Mac, co-enjoying a deck-christening brandy old-fashioned or two, when I announced that if I was anointed King of our subdivision, I would outlaw noisy power mowers like his, because it drove me crazy listening to the thing ruining the quiet beauty of early summer evenings and early summer days. Mac sat up in his chair – his voice rising – and said if that was the case, he would become a criminal, serial, law-breaking citizen for the first time in his life. And, I said – my voice rising – if that was the case, I would have the painful responsibility of seeing him summarily executed in a public space for all the community to see. At that point Mac fell silent, then excused himself, and left me sitting alone on his spanking new deck staring at my drink.

"I don't see you and Mac talking over the fence these days," MaryLou, my wife, said a couple of days later.

"Not as much as we used to," I said.

"What's up?" she asked, looking up from the dirty dishes. "You guys fighting?"

"I guess we just drifted apart."

"I always wondered what you two talked about all these years."

"Sports mostly," I said, "and his lawn."

"His beloved lawn," MaryLou said, which was as close to sarcasm as she gets.

It was Mac's beloved lawn. Fixing up that lawn with his wife Betsy was one of the few things left to fill the long hours of retirement, I guess. He would mow two, sometimes three times a week at the peak of the season, always making that diagonal cut pattern that's become popular in recent years. In the spring and the fall, the green truck with butterflies and little kids playing in a field of flowers painted on its side would pull up to their place, and a guy with a protective mask and gloves would get out and spray fertilizer and deadly poisons on the lawn to induce the miracle of life.

"What'ya think of that lawn?" Mac would say to any neighbor who was passing by, as Betsy stood there with the string trimmer in hand. "She's the best girl a man could want," he would add, nodding in Betsy's direction.

In the winter, out of concern for the mailman and the rare pedestrian, Mac and Betsy would work as a team, snowblowing the walk and chopping away glare ice that laid in wait on the sidewalk in front of their house. Time was catching up with the two of them; they were both bent over and creaky. Still, there they were, hammering and chipping away with parkas zipped up to the chin. But, doing your duty wasn't the same as the lawn; only the lawn was a work of art or something, so the two of them greeted the spring with more joy than a duck on a rainy morning.

"What a day, huh?" Mac would shout over at me as he cranked up the mower for the first pass. "Spring has sprung!" Betsy would always say, and that was the start of the season for me. But, that lawn, why did they care? What did they get out of it?

"How would I know?" MaryLou said when I asked for her two cents' worth. "Lawns are a man thing."

"I'm a man, and I don't get it," I said.

"Give me my flower garden; you guys can have your green rectangles," MaryLou said. "Don't ask me."

I tried to slip the issue in with our neighbor Jean, who was known for keeping tabs on the comings and goings on our block. I said something about how much time Mac put in on lawn care and she ignored that.

"Is that St. Rita's?" she asked, pointing in the air where the sound of church bells was floating over us. "Is there a funeral service today?"

"A James Burns, I think I read," I answered.

"Did you know him?" Jean asked. "I know what his wife looks like – sits in the third pew on the right. That's the fourth funeral this month," she said. "I used to love the sound of church bells," she added with a shrug.

The summer was a dry one that year, and everyone's lawn turned to straw, except Mac's and Fred's on the kitty corner, who said his dad had been a "lawn nut" and that was why he was one too. On both sides of the street, six lawns in a row baked to a deathly white, flanked by the two green plots on the ends. From June on, the grass kept bleaching, and St. Rita's bells kept ringing as Mac watered and mowed, watered and mowed, on weekdays and Sundays, at dawn and at dusk. Then one day, MaryLou and I looked out and saw Betsy leaning into the mower all alone.

"What's up?" MaryLou asked.

"Beats me," I said, squinting between the curtains. "I'm sure the sun came up yesterday, the tides are probably going in and out on the coasts, the moon is still orbiting around..."

"I get it," MaryLou said.

"I'll ask Jean what she knows," I said.

"No point in that," MaryLou said. "No more of this shillyshallying. I'll just call Betsy."

It turned out Mac had done something to his hip and was confined to sitting and marginal limping for the rest of the summer. Betsy told MaryLou, cutting their thick lawn had just about killed her, and since young kids no longer hire out to cut grass like when we were young, she didn't know where to turn. MaryLou volunteered me.

"What the hell?" I said.

"You've got the time now," MaryLou said. "You're among the newly retired, remember?"

"That's right," I said. "I'm no spring chicken. Found my first liver spot on my right hand today."

MaryLou flinched at that comment, since she had just sprouted her own aging spot and didn't like it one bit. For the most part, she didn't look her age.

"Besides," I said, "it'd be awkward, me going over there. "

"Whatever it was between you two, get over it," MaryLou said in her no uncertain terms tone of voice. I took a couple of days to think about it, but bolstered by her courage, on a hot July day, I retraced the old familiar steps to Mac's house. Betsy greeted me at the door with her usual smile, which was a relief.

"You're the cavalry to the rescue, that's for sure," she said. "I've been watering early mornings and at the end of the day, but the mowing is more than I can handle. We're a little too strapped for money to hire one of those mowing companies. Of course, we don't expect you to do this for nothing."

I said what were neighbors for, and she walked me through the air-conditioned house, past the shrine of photos of the grandkids, to the back deck where Mac sat huddled under a sun umbrella, staring out at the lawn. He turned at the sound of the sliding door and winced with pain. I walked over.

"Well, well," Mac said. "His honor the King."

"Look, Mac," I started to say, but he cut me off with a wave and motioned to a lawn chair that rested in the glare of the sun. "What's this," I said, "the hot box?"

"Public execution for all the community to see," Mac said, his memory as sharp as ever. "Kinda funny, isn't it, you coming over to use my noisy mower? If you're smart, you'll do the front first, then take a break, then do the back. It's a bitcher today. And don't try and do diagonals. That takes practice, and you'd just screw it up. Betsy'll show you where the stuff is. You'd better get going before the sun fries your butt."

The sun seemed to be rising faster than normal that day. Like always, Mac's aging mower rattled and buzzed like a muffler on its last, fatal trip to the shop. As I made my first passes on the lawn, I cursed MaryLou and cursed myself and dreamed dreams of revenge, like setting the cut lower so the green would burn brown in the sun. But, I didn't. The lawn was especially long and the sweat poured down my temples until my short sleeves were soaked from mopping my face. Just to show Mac, I cut diagonal after diagonal, lining them up in perfect parallel patterns, the edge of one row barely overlapping with the next. With all the watering Betsy had done, plus the late summer sun, the grass glowed a deep green, shimmering in the light breeze before it was cut, laying flat and well-shaped when I finished a row. The freshly mowed grass smelled sweet in the air. When I got done mowing the front, I took the string trimmer and cleaned up the edges along the perimeters, around the trees and up against the shrubs where Mac and Betsy were sometimes a little sloppy for my taste. Then I stepped back, spotted a few places where I had missed, clipped them, grabbed a broom and swept any loose clippings off the sidewalks in front and up to the house. As I paused to look at my work, a cloud shaded the sun and a cool breeze softened the air and refreshed me. It was a job well done, the ripe green lawn looked alive and well against the straw white yards that surrounded it. After a minute, I walked toward the back yard.

"Take a load off," Mac said as I sat down again in the lawn chair. He pointed to a lemonade on the deck table. "You look like you could use a glass. Did you hear the church bells a minute ago?" he asked. "It's been a busy summer."

"Hearing and that mower of yours don't go together," I said.

"Look," Mac said, "if I could find a kid to do this, I wouldn't put you through the torture."

"Kids are all at their computer screens," I said. "Lemonade never tasted this good," I added, raising my glass in the air. "How's the hip?"

"There are twenty-four mowings left this year, and I'm not going to be able to do a damn one, if that's what you're getting at," he said.

"That's not what I meant," I said.

"To answer your question, the heat helps," Mac said, pointing to his hip, "but it still hurts like a son of a bitch some days. The low points in my life are coming down with this thing, the day they downsized my job after fifty years of loyal service, and my resulting first day as a crossing guard at the grade school. But life goes on, right? How about those Indians? I smell a pennant."

After some awkward negotiations, Betsy got MaryLou and I to agree to go out for what Betsy called "a romantic getaway dinner" on them once a month in payment for my work on the lawn. So, I was locked into two visits a week, what with Betsy watering like crazy and the fertilizer chemicals pushing the grass up faster than you can oil a mower. Before long, we had a regular routine – Mac, Betsy and I, sitting on the deck during my break between the front and back and sometimes at the end of my work too. We'd talk about different things, like kids and getting old, and they'd reminisce about old times or how their young neighbors didn't talk over the fence as much as people used to. Sometimes we'd just sit and watch the shadows move across the deck at the end of the day. The first couple times we shared lemonade, then we graduated to a beer or an appropriate summer cocktail to the point that MaryLou started to look at me funny when I got home.

"What's going on over there?" she asked me. "You looped?"

"Pleasantly high," I said.

"Your visits keep getting longer and longer."

"What's this all about?" I asked.

"I'm just saying, what does it say that you're over there so much?"

"It wouldn't be polite to just mow and run," I explained. "Besides, they're good people with some good ideas about life and things. They talked about having you over one of these times. I didn't think you'd want to. We get on sports topics sometimes, and I know how you feel about that. So I made an excuse."

"You don't know how I feel. I sometimes talk sports. Besides, there must be other things the three of you talk about. When's Mac going to be back on his feet, anyway?"

"Not this mowing season, that's for sure. Where do you want to go for this month's dinner date?" I asked, reminding her of the payoff for my new job.

....

Mac, Betsy, and I were just getting into the cocktail phase of the day when we were joined by their son, Raymond. I had seen Raymond grow up from a distance, but never got to know him all that well, since we had girls and there was an age gap that kept the kids from becoming friends.

"I suppose you're wondering why I don't come over and cut the ancestral lawn?" Raymond asked me as he accepted his Pina Colada from Betsy. I started to say something, but he interrupted and said that "they" – his parents – knew where he stood on the lawn, which was that spending time watering and cutting grass was a pure waste of time. He called this an honest difference of opinion between them and said, with a smile on his face, it apparently was an honest difference with me too. I then asked him if he had an honest difference with us over the need to shovel snow off the sidewalk in winter, but, before he could answer, Betsy said something about how busy Raymond was and then asked him how their grandkids were doing in school.

"Straight A's," Raymond said. "Sue and I were talking about bringing them over to see you next weekend, or the week after."

"You'll have to admit the old lawn looks pretty damn good?" I said when a silence ensued after this exchange, and Raymond just laughed a private joke kind of laugh before draining his drink and taking his leave a short time later. Raymond had worked his way through school and gone on to become a lawyer, which made him the apple of his parents' eye, since most of us on the block had humbler jobs than that. I knew how they felt about him because I had been hearing their stories of Raymond's achievements and ideas on life during our patio breaks. When Raymond drove off in his sedan, I saw Betsy beaming and Mac repeated something about how busy Raymond was and how he didn't expect him to have time for doing their lawn, but it was great to see him for a change.

"By the way," Mac said when we had settled back down to drinking our drinks and looking out at the back yard, "were you saying the lawn looks better now than it used to? For one thing, you're edging is too close. It's gonna burn out and look crappy brown all along the front."

"Give the man a break," Betsy said. "The price is right and the company is welcome," to which Mac raised his cocktail in the air and nodded a small nod of agreement.

....

I tried to describe to MaryLou what I thought I had witnessed that day, about Raymond and his smart- Alec attitude and how disrespectful it seemed to me, but she wouldn't listen.

Bamboo Scoops *By Willy Conley*

"I don't understand this," she said. "Even in the old days, when you and Mac talked over the fence, all I heard from you was complaints about how loud his mower was and how stubborn he was in his opinions. And now it's 'Betsy says' and 'Mac and Betsy don't do it that way.'"

"You're the one who volunteered me for duty," I said.

"I didn't put you up for adoption," she said.

"As for Mac, in the old days maybe I just didn't have enough facts to reach a sound judgment," I said. "Nothing says a person can't change his mind about something, does it? Plus, he knows his sports."

"This is a seismic change in the weather," MaryLou said.

"I still don't say Mac is perfect. For example, I think he's actually a little pissed at how good I've fixed up the yard."

"Good to know he isn't perfect," MaryLou said. So I gave her a hug and she half smiled, but then pulled away to go into the kitchen and make supper.

....

The news of Raymond's divorce hit Mac and Betsy hard. It didn't go over good when I said it was a common thing these days. Betsy stared daggers at me and Mac straightened up in his chair to where he let out a groan from the hip pain.

"We didn't see it coming," Betsy said. "Not a hint, not a clue, the kids seemed happy, everything was going fine. Where did this come from?"

"What did we do wrong, that's what you're asking, isn't it?" Mac said.

"Don't start in on that again, Mac," Betsy said.

"I don't think this is the place to discuss this," Mac said, nodding his head in my direction.

"No one's at fault in these things..." I started in, but Mac gave me a look this time and the two of them went back to discussing the divorce like I wasn't sitting there on the deck with them, drink in hand, watching the sun set like we had so many times this summer. I tried to take advantage of a lull in their conversation by mentioning that fall was in the air and then joking "I'm not raking," but it fell flat.

....

"You can't fix all their problems and mow their lawn," MaryLou said when I told her. "'Into each life', not to be callous. I suppose I could take over some pound cake, if you think that would help."

As the leaves turned and the lawn went into its inevitable decline, the refreshment schedule on the back deck got erratic. Betsy sometimes sitting there silent and serving nothing at all, and other times bringing out double and triple shot cocktails that she and Mac would put away like a glass of ice water. Sometimes the talk flowed like always; other times there were long silences I just sat through and waited to end.

"Sounds like it's getting uncomfortable," Mary Lou said. "Maybe the timing is good, what with the mowing year coming to an end."

I said the mowing season wasn't over yet, but I knew it almost was. After some thought, I decided it might be good to mark the end of the season with a cookout. I proposed fixing my special barbecue chicken at our house and taking it over to Mac's deck for a fall salute to the lawn.

"You think?" MaryLou asked. "We've been neighbors a long time and I like them, but the three of you, maybe it should just be you?"

I brushed that aside and said it wouldn't be a party without her and she said okay. I made the call.

"I don't know," Betsy said over the phone. "I'll check with Mac, but his hip has been worse than ever lately."

"The work's on us," I said. "You just provide your deck and leave the rest to me and MaryLou. It'll do you guys good," I added, and then remembered how my attempts at advice had gone over in the past.

"I'll let you know," Betsy said with no further ado.

"I'd say it's fifty-fifty," I said to MaryLou, who looked more relieved than anything to my eyes. But just when you think you know people, they fool you.

"Mac says yes," Betsy said over the phone. "Our deck, our drinks, your food. How does Friday night sound?"

The weather gave us a break that Friday. It was one of those Indian Summer blessings – warm and dry with enough wind to start the maple leaves falling out of the sky like a red shower. MaryLou spent the morning making her potato salad with the secret ingredient of sliced radishes; when she vacated the kitchen, I marinated the chicken, stoked up the grill and slow smoked a nice mix of white and dark meat to cover our bases with the unknown tastes of our hosts. I suggested to MaryLou some conversation topics that I thought we should avoid that night and got cold stares on that. When the time came, we got dressed up more than usual and walked over, Greeks bearing gifts. Betsy welcomed us and guided us into the kitchen where she had laid out knit warming pads for the food to rest on.

"These are pretty," MaryLou said, fingering the pads. "Did you make these yourself?" she asked, and Betsy said yes, it was one of her hobbies that passed the time. Then Betsy took us out to the deck, walking with a noticeable limp she said was sciatica acting up worse than usual. Mac struggled out of his chair to greet MaryLou with some formality and ushered us to our lawn chairs in the fading sun.

"I see what you three had going for you here with this beautiful deck," MaryLou said shading her eyes from the early evening glare. "We could use a nice set-up like this ourselves," she said, glancing in my direction.

"Got it done just in time for the sit-down phase of our lives," Mac said, but then smiled and passed Betsy's hot hors d' oeuvres to MaryLou while Betsy distributed the featured cocktail of the evening.

"I was sorry to hear about Raymond," MaryLou started in, breaking the first conversation hint I had given her that morning.

"Don't worry about that boy," Mac said. "He's landing on his feet. Got a girlfriend already, nice girl with a good job and a teenage boy. You should see him, a big kid, an athlete."

"It's the grandkids we're most worried about," Betsy said.

"The innocent victims," MaryLou said. "It's always roughest on them, isn't it?"

"Victims?" Mac said.

"It's just an expression, Mac," Betsy said, turning her drink bottoms up and gesturing in our direction to see if we needed refills. When we declined, she said she'd slow down on the next one but was trying to numb the sciatica in the bud. While she was gone, Mac turned on the charm with MaryLou.

"How come this husband of yours never brought you over to decorate our cocktail hours?" he asked.

"You'll have to ask him," MaryLou said. "I thought maybe it was a secret lawn society ritual or something," she said. "You know, celebrating the harvest like the native cultures do."

"Celebrating?" Mac said. "Maybe there's something to that. A good lawn is something to treasure, that's sure. And while we're on the subject," he continued as Betsy rejoined us, new drink in hand, "we – both of us – want to thank you for loaning us your husband for the summer."

"Cheers to that," Betsy chimed in. "I'm not sure what we would have done without him. For that matter, what we'll do next year, this fall, this winter..."

"What Betsy means," Mac broke in, "is the long-range plans are a little fuzzy right now."

"Maybe Raymond can come over and help you out now that he's got fewer obligations?" I said.

"Raymond just got another promotion," Mac replied. "The law is not exactly an idle profession, you know."

"I think this is something for them to work out," MaryLou said to me. Then she and Betsy stood up to go get the food, and Mac and I sat there and traveled down memory lane and talked sports until the women returned. As the two of them set out the colored paper plates and my chicken, Mac lit a couple of those mosquito repelling candles around the perimeter of the deck, giving the whole place a kind of spooky glow, complete with swaying cobweb shadows on the deck floor. In front of us, out on the darkening lawn, lightning bugs flashed on and off every couple of seconds and then the St. Rita's bells rang out in the air.

"There they are again," Mac said, pointing to the sky. "Sometimes I wish my hearing was even worse than it is," he said, downing a shot of his drink.

"A good dose of reality never hurt anyone," Betsy said. "Besides, that's seven o'clock mass."

"That's my Betsy!" Mac said, raising his cocktail glass into the flickering light of the insect bombs. "Whenever I start to whine, she slaps me up the side of the head and we trudge on."

"You guys have something special," MaryLou said, sounding not like herself, but sounding like she meant what she was saying. "So, tell me," she went on, "what did the three of you discuss at your lawn parties this summer?"

"Different things," Betsy said. "It might be something Father Couch said on Sunday, maybe laughing about raising kids, sometimes just enjoying the summer weather."

"Us, maybe?" MaryLou said, looking over at me in the dim light.

"You? Oh no," Betsy said. "Sometimes we talked about the neighbors, mostly stuff we heard first from Jean. Not about you. Why would you think that?"

"It just crossed my mind, I guess," MaryLou said.

"We observe all the basic delicacies of civilized conversation around here," Mac said, waving a chicken bone in the air as he talked. "We have our tact intact," he said and laughed.

At this point in the evening we all dove into chicken and potato salad like no tomorrow. Mac and Betsy carried the conversational load pretty much by themselves, laughing like they often did about the old days in their house, talking about the grandkids, almost sounding like they were wrapping up a time in their lives.

"A lotta years," Betsy said at one point and Mac seconded her.

"Good years," he agreed as the lightening bugs kept sparking out on the lawn. "It's been a good home, here," Mac said. "Raised the kids, buried our dog..."

"Buddy!" Betsy broke in. "What a little guy that was. I still miss that dog. Say, we aren't giving you two much chance to talk, are we?" she asked MaryLou.

"It's all right," MaryLou said. "I like listening to the two of you."

"You've got a peach there," Mac said to me, and I said "You got that right" as loud as my voice would carry.

Dessert arrived and then the mosquitoes finally fought their way through the bug bombs, so we all raised our glasses in one last toast and declared it a night. MaryLou and I bundled up our serving plates, exchanged hugs with Betsy and a handshake with Mac and headed on home.

"Those two are the salt of the earth," MaryLou said as we walked through the darkness.

"What do you mean?" I asked.

"I don't know," MaryLou said. "They just have something. I can't name it, there's just something there. Between them."

"They don't always get along, I can tell you that having had the experience," I said, but she just shrugged her shoulders as we reached our front steps. "I'll get the dishes," I said, and MaryLou nodded and headed off to bed.

That night turned out to be a swan song of sorts. Mac and Betsy got through the fall raking season with the help of one of those noisy leaf blowers, and by the time the first snowfall hit, they had moved out of their home to a senior living place that was suited to their declining physical condition. I said a brief goodbye to them, with Mac cutting the visit short before there was a chance for anyone to get too emotional. A young couple with three kids moved into their home, and come spring the guy was out there mowing the lawn with the damn mower that Mac must have thrown in with the house. It's as loud as ever, but I don't care, as long as that lawn is a glowing green every summer, poisons and all. My lawn will never be in the same league with that one, since one of the few things MaryLou and I agree on these days is the evils of lawn chemicals. I've made plans to visit Mac and Betsy at the nursing home I don't know how many times, but so far have put it off. MaryLou sometimes urges me to go.

"It'd do them good. It'd do you good, "she says, the irritation in her voice clear as ever.

To me, I don't have to go. I can see them in my mind, a little more bent with the passing days, every shocking new breakdown in their bodies taking them by surprise. They're going to need walkers and then electric carts to get them down to the dining hall soon, but they'll attend daily Mass and soldier on because Betsy won't allow much griping no matter what. I know Raymond doesn't come often so the grandkids don't visit, but Mac and Betsy agree on their excuses for that and that's good. MaryLou and I could use a few more comfortable lies between us for sure. Maybe I'll visit them one of these days, I imagine some days as pretty lonely there, although into each life that particular rain is going to fall. Maybe I'll drop by, maybe not. We'll see what the future brings.

EsCAPET *By Sarah Katharina Kayß*

Touch

By Cynthia Ris

—on Giotto's Resurrection

She reaches out, moonlight golden
on her draped head, but he holds her

at more than arm's length: noli me tangere—
the words waver on the flag he grips.

He's been through so much—the taunts,
the beatings, nails that split bones—

he couldn't bear even a touch. His disciples
swoon with the loss of him. Behind them,

angels smile, accustomed to what it's like
to live beyond touch. Still, she reaches toward him,

wants to hold him, to give him what her pale hands
can help him remember. He steadies himself

against the rock wall, gazes at her shining face.
Stars wink in the checkered sky.

The Sheep and the Shepherd

By Matthew Popadiuk

Oh, little lamb
So meek and mild
As God is gentle
As I was as a child
But now I'm grown
And you are too
And I want little lamb
Again, to be like you
For God made you
And God made me
So teach me little lamb
To be just like thee
Oh, teach me little lamb
Teach me to trust
Before I am ashes
Before I am dust
And help me to live
Your every word
For I am the sheep
And you, the shepherd

With Each Step You Take

By Matthew Popadiuk

I offer you my shoulder
To wipe away your tears
I hold you in my arms
To calm all your fears

I sit and I listen to you
If and when you need an ear
And whenever you need me
Rest assured I will be near

Your hopes and dreams I share
And your triumph and despair
Your worries too, when blue
Because, for you, I care

I think of you often
So we are never apart
And to keep you close by
I hold you in my heart

And so, I would do anything
So to make you smile
As with each step you take
I walk with you, every mile

What Becomes of the Fallen Angels?

By Mary Shanley

What becomes of the fallen angels?
Do they ever find their way
back into grace?
Or have they forgotten
they once had wings,
and now simply use legs
to cart themselves around
the spheres of this
here creation?

Can one recognize a fallen angel
on a Saturday, at three in the afternoon
at Tower Records?

Do they gravitate to the gospel
music section because
they have a deep yearning
in the pit of their souls
for their former glory days,
when they serenaded
the creator of all things
in the holiest of
holy sanctuaries?

Or do they just strut
around the entire
store, dripping with
fierce attitude
and finally
leave without
even buying one
single record.

Do fallen angels slip
into Grace Church
and silently sit in the

last row with their
heads bowed for
ten minutes or so,
or are they
irreverent critters
who bounce around the city
in hot shot sneakers,
looking for some fast
action they can
sink their teeth into.

I wonder if any of my friends
are fallen angels?
In fact, I could be
one myself,
shuffling around
this earth scene
for two or three lifetimes,
until I develop a
higher soprano
or a funkier falsetto,
so I can finally bop back
behind the curtain,
where heaven is
currently in progress
and find my way
back to the place
especially reserved
for me.

I sure hope there's enough
room for my new boom
box back there.

Sea Out *By Eleanor Bennet*

Contributor Profiles

Literary Contributors

Valentina Cano is a student of classical singing who spends her free time either writing or reading. Her works have appeared in Exercise Bowler, Blinking Cursor, Theory Train, Cartier Street Press, Berg Gasse 19, Precious Metals, A Handful of Dust, The Scarlet Sound, The Adroit Journal, Perceptions Literary Magazine, Welcome to Wherever, The Corner Club Press, Death Rattle, Danse Macabre, Subliminal Interiors, Generations Literary Journal, Super Poetry Highway, Stream Press, Stone Telling, Popshot, Golden Sparrow Literary Review, Rem Magazine, Structo, The 22 Magazine, The Black Fox Literary Magazine, Niteblade, Tuck Magazine, Ontologica, Congruent Spaces Magazine, Pipe Dream, Decades Review, Anatomy, Lowestof Chronicle, Muddy River Poetry Review, Lady Ink Magazine, White Masquerade Anthology and Perhaps I'm Wrong About the World. You can find her here: http://carabosseslibrary.blogspot.com

John Cullen attended SUNY Geneseo and currently lives in West Michigan. In the past, he has worked as a driveway repairman and at a talent agency, but he currently teaches in Michigan. His other poems have appeared in Controlled Burn, The MacGuffin, and The Cincinnati Poetry Review.

Francis DiClemente lives in Syracuse, New York, where he works as a video producer. In his spare time he writes and takes photographs. He is the author of Outskirts of Intimacy, a poetry chapbook published by Flutter Press.

Rick Hartwell is a retired middle school (remember, the hormonally-challenged?) English teacher living in Moreno Valley, California with his wife of thirty-six years (poor soul, her, not him), their disabled daughter, one of their sons and his ex-wife and their two children, and twelve cats. Yes, twelve! He believes in the succinct, that the small becomes large; and, like the Transcendentalists and William Blake, that the instant contains eternity. Given his "druthers," if he's not writing poetry, Rick would rather still be tailing plywood in a mill in Oregon.

Karen K. Hugg's fiction, non-fiction and translations have appeared in Hip Mama, Soul's Road, Specs, The Pitkin Review, Opium, Poetry East, Shifting Borders, Northwest Garden News, and Desert Dog. She has an M.A. from the

University of Illinois and an M.F.A. from Goddard College. She was born in Chicago, has lived in Tucson and now lives in a forested suburb of Seattle. She just completed a novel and is beginning a memoir about adopting three children from Poland. When not writing, she works as a gardener. She can be reached at karenhugg at gmail dot com.

Jon Kolb is presently Assistant Grandchild Babysitter reporting directly to his wife, Donna. He recently completed a crime novel (unpublished and looking for a home) and has had several plays performed by local (Milwaukee, WI) theaters.

Don Kunz taught literature, creative writing, and film studies at the University of Rhode Island for 36 years. His essays, poems, and short stories have appeared in over sixty literary journals. Don has retired to Bend, Oregon, where he writes fiction and poetry, volunteers, studies Spanish, and is learning to play the Native American Flute.

Kaye Linden has an MFA in fiction, is an editor with the Bacopa Literary Review, assistant editor for Soundings Review and fiction teacher at Santa Fe College, Gainesville. Shelfstealers.com has contracted to publish her collection: "Fifty Tales from Ma's Watering Hole." Kaye was nominated in 2011 for a Pushcart prize. Her stories have been published in multiple journals including, but not limited to, The Raven Chronicles, Six Minute Stories, The Linnets Wings, Soundings Review, Bacopa Literary Review, the Feathered Flounder, Drunk Monkeys anthology #2. Visit her at www.kayelinden.com and sign up for her blog: http://shelfstealers.com/watchkayelindenwrite/.

Kathryn (Nordan) Lynch is currently studying Liberal Arts with a Teaching Specialization at Northern Virginia Community College. In addition to her studies, she is employed on-campus as a tutor, assisting fellow students with both math and writing. In NVCC's 2012 writing contest, she was awarded second place for her short story "Heroes Among Us," which was published in the school's literary journal The Walrus.

Mira Martin-Parker is currently pursuing an MFA in creative writing at San Francisco State University. Her work has appeared in Diverse Voices Quarterly, Istanbul Literary Review, Literary Bohemian, The Minetta Review, The Monarch Review, Mythium, Ragazine, Tattoo Highway, Yellow Medicine Review, and Zyzzyva.

Bob Meszaros taught English at Hamden High School in Hamden, Connecticut, for thirty-two years. He retired from high school teaching in June of 1999. During the 1970s and early 80s his poetry appeared in a number of literary journals, such as En Passant and Voices International. In the year 2000 he began once again to submit his work for publication. His poems have subsequently appeared in The Connecticut Review, Main Street Rag, Tar River Poetry, Concho River Review, Innisfree and other literary journals. He is now writing (both poetry and prose) about his many years of public school teaching.

Lance Nizami has no formal training in the arts. He is active in the world's most competitive profession, yet without an institutional appointment or income. He started writing poetry during a long airplane flight in 2010, and has written much since then in-flight. As of 8 May 2012 he has 64 poems in print or in press.

Richard Peake published early poems in Impetus alongside John Ciardi and in The Georgia Review. Collections of his poetry include Wings Across... and Poems for Terence published by Vision Press. He published Birds and Other Beasts in 2007. Recent poems have appeared in Avocet, Asinine Poetry, Boundless 2011 and 2012, Ides of March, Nature Croons, Raven Images, Skive, Sol Magazine and Shine Journal (one nominated for the Pushcart Prize), The Road Not Taken, The Dead Mule, The Texas Poetry Calendar 2012 and elsewhere. A life-long naturalist, a father and grandfather, he teaches birds, Shakespeare, and writing in Osher Lifelong Learning Institute.

Matthew Popadiuk is a New York based poet whose first chapbook will be released this summer. His poetry is influenced by his Ukrainian heritage and the poets of the Romantic Period.

Cynthia Nitz Ris, a former attorney, freelance journalist, and photographer, teaches English at the University of Cincinnati and works as a freelance editor. Some of her poetry has appeared in poem, home: An Anthology of Ars Poetica, The Innisfree Poetry Journal, and Identity Theory. This work, along with her non-fiction prose and a novel in-progress, reflects interest in identity, justice, spirituality, nature, travel, children—including her three sons, and the arts. Author of the composition reader, Law and Order.

Yvette A. Schnoeker-Shorb's poetry has appeared in Spectrum, Wilderness House Literary Review, Terrain.org: A Journal of the Built and Natural

Environments, Concho River Review, Pedestal Magazine, Evening Street Review, Midwest Quarterly, Wild Earth, Jelly Bucket, Red River Review, and other journals. Her current social research and interests include the phenomenon of biophilia related to sustainable practices and human interaction with the natural world. She holds an interdisciplinary MA and is co-founder of Native West Press--a 501(c)(3) nonprofit natural history press (which recently published the anthology What's Nature Got to Do with Me? Staying Wildly Sane in a Mad World).

Mary Shanley is a poet/writer/musician. She began writing songs, then poems then stories. She wanders inside and outside her head and writes about it. She drinks espresso and discusses any and everything in her orbit at any particular time.

Patty Somlo has been nominated for the Pushcart Prize three times and was a finalist in the Tom Howard Short Story Contest. Her first collection, From Here to There and Other Stories, was published by Paraguas Books. Her work has appeared in the Los Angeles Review, the Santa Clara Review, the Jackson Hole Review, WomenArts Quarterly, Guernica, Slow Trains, Shaking Magazine, The Write Room and Fringe Magazine, among others, and in several anthologies. Look for her upcoming work in Evening Street Review, Kudzu Review, Slow Trains, Gemini Magazine and Red Ochre Lit.

Crystal Lane Swift (PhD, Rhetoric and Public Address, LSU, 2008) is a communication Professor at Mt. San Antonio College and California State University, Northridge. Her poetry has appeared in a number of anthologies. She has published an academic book, This House Would Ethically Engage (2008), over 15 academic articles (2005-2011), and a book of poetry, God Bless Paul (2008). She has produced three films: Sculpting the Rhetorician (2005), Debating Christianity from Below (2005), and It's Never About a Boy (2011), and an album, On Going Battle (2011). She lives in Hollywood, CA with her best friend, Elba Soto-Quinones. (www.crystallaneswift.com).

Jessica Tyner is originally from Oregon, a member of the Cherokee Nation, and has been a writer and editor for ten years. Currently, she is a copy writer for Word Jones, a travel writer with Mucha Costa Rica, a writer for TripFab, a copy editor at the London-based Flaneur Arts Journal, and a contributing editor at New York's Thalo Magazine. She has recently published short fiction in India's Out of Print Magazine, and poetry in Slow Trains Literary Journal, Straylight

Magazine, Solo Press, and Glint Literary Journal. She lives in San José, Costa Rica.

Kirby Wright was born and raised in Honolulu, Hawaii. He is a graduate of Punahou School in Honolulu and the University of California at San Diego. He received his MFA in Creative Writing from San Francisco State University. Wright has been nominated for two Pushcart Prizes and is a past recipient of the Ann Fields Poetry Prize, the Academy of American Poets Award, the Browning Society Award for Dramatic Monologue, and Arts Council Silicon Valley Fellowships in Poetry and The Novel. BEFORE THE CITY, his first book of poetry, took First Place at the 2003 San Diego Book Awards. Wright is also the author of the companion novels PUNAHOU BLUES and MOLOKA'I NUI AHINA, both set in Hawaii. He was a Visiting Fellow at the 2009 International Writers Conference in Hong Kong, where he represented the Pacific Rim region of Hawaii. He was the 2011 Artist in Residence at Milkwood International, Czech Republic.

Art Contributor Profiles

Eleanor Leonne Bennett is a 16 year old internationally award winning photographer and artist who has won first places with National Geographic,The World Photography Organisation, Nature's Best Photography, Papworth Trust, Mencap, The Woodland trust and Postal Heritage. Her photography has been published in the Telegraph , The Guardian, BBC News Website and on the cover of books and magazines in the United states and Canada. www.eleanorleonnebennett.zenfolio.com

Emily K. Bright's poetry has appeared in multiple journals and anthologies, including North American Review, Other Voices International, and Beloved on Earth: 150 Poems of Grief and Gratitude. Her chapbook Glances Back is available from Pudding House Press. This is her artistic debut.

Willy Conley is a Registered Biological Photographer who has worked a number of years in the field of biomedical photography at: University of Texas Medical Branch, Cedars-Sinai Medical Center, Johns Hopkins University, and Yale University. A graduate of the Rochester Institute of Technology, his photographs have been published in: American Photographer, Industrial Photography, Deaf World, Deaf American Poetry, Rio Grande Review,

Kaleidoscope, 34th Parallel, and The Antietam Review, to name a few. Although no longer working as a medical photographer, he continues to enjoy shooting, exhibiting, and publishing photos. He is currently a professor of Theatre Arts at Gallaudet University, the world's only liberal arts university for deaf and hard-of-hearing students, in Washington, D.C. To review more of his photographic work, please visit: www.willyconley.com.

Leah Givens is a former photographer for The Red and Black, the newspaper of The University of Georgia. She has since earned her M.D. from Washington University School of Medicine in St. Louis. She worked for several years in Alzheimer's research and continues to photograph as well as write. Her work has appeared in The Colored Lens, Penduline Press, and Poydras Review and is upcoming in The Bellingham Review. Her website is http://www.leahgivens.com.

Nathan Healy is what you might call a "newcomer" to the photography world. After years of taking photos, he has decided to pursue this passion.

Sarah Katharina Kayß of Koblenz (Germany) has a B.A. in History and Comparative Religion (Ruhr University of Bochum), M.A. in Modern History (King's College, University of London), and her artwork, essays and poetry have appeared in literary magazines, journals and anthologies in Germany, Switzerland, Austria, the United Kingdom, Canada, New Zealand and the United States. Sarah edits the bilingual magazine PostPoetry, A Literary Magazine. She lives, studies and works in London

Nina Snowden is a retired schoolteacher. Her novel, In and Out of Madness, is available on Amazon. Her art and photography, published in literary magazines, has also won awards and been sold all over the South. She wrote a column about the life of a published author for a California e-zine called Active Voice. She also does book reviews for the Alabama Writers' Forum Online Reviews, and she writes articles dealing with mental illness for the newspaper, New York City Voices. She has had short stories published in two literary magazines and in four different anthologies. One story won first place at the Baldwin County Writers Fiction contest. Dee Jordan AKA Nina Snowden www.inandoutofmadness.net.

www.ingramcontent.com/pod-product-compliance
Ingram Content Group UK Ltd.
Pitfield, Milton Keynes, MK11 3LW, UK
UKHW041916190726
13854UKWH00003B/1272

9 781105 849305